Contents

KU-273-840

Lots of love from Gran

Chapter One

The sun, a blazing red ball of heat, rose swiftly over the plains of Africa, heralding the dawn. It was the start of a new day and all the animals could sense that something special was about to happen.

They came walking, flying, running and crawling across the plains – rhinoceroses, cheetahs, storks, elephants, flamingos, giraffes and even ants – to gather around Pride Rock. There they watched and waited in silence.

An elderly baboon called Rafiki

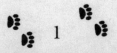

hobbled past the other animals, leaning on his walking stick as he went. He climbed on to the top of Pride Rock, where Mufasa, Sarabi and their new-born cub, Simba, were waiting for him. Rafiki had been looking forward to this moment for a long, long time.

The King of the Pride Lands, Mufasa, was a big, powerful lion with a full, shaggy mane. But his face was a picture of tenderness as he gazed at his new-born son, cradled in his wife's paws.

Rafiki smiled down at Simba. He took the melon he was carrying, broke it open and smeared the juice on the lion cub's forehead. Then he took Simba from his mother and carried him to the edge of Pride Rock. Rafiki lifted the cub high into the air and the hundreds of animals bowed low and cheered their future King.

Each and every animal who lived in the Pride Lands had come to greet Simba that day and pledge their loyalty – all except one. Scar, Mufasa's brother and Simba's uncle, was sulking in a cave. He had managed to trap a mouse and was playing with it cruelly as it struggled to get free.

'Life's not fair, is it?' he grumbled. 'Now I shall never be King.' He scooped up the mouse and held it in his paw, smirking at it. 'And you will never see the light of day again!'

He was about to pop the mouse into his mouth when a voice behind him squawked, 'Didn't your mother ever tell you not to play with your food?'

Scar stopped in surprise and the mouse seized the opportunity to escape. Zazu, the African hornbill who was Mufasa's major-domo, flew down and landed in front of Scar.

'King Mufasa's on his way,' he announced, 'so you'd better have a good excuse for missing the ceremony this morning.'

'You made me lose my lunch, Zazu,' Scar retorted rudely.

'You'll lose more than that when the King gets hold of you,' Zazu warned. 'He's as mad as a hippo with a hernia.'

'Oh, I quiver with fear!' Scar said sarcastically, and advanced towards

Zazu, who looked decidedly nervous.

'Now, Scar, don't stare at me that way,' he stammered. 'Help!'

Scar scooped Zazu up into his mouth just as King Mufasa strode into the cave.

'Drop him!' he roared.

Sulkily, Scar spat Zazu out. 'Why, if it isn't my big brother,' he sneered.

Mufasa stared coldly at Scar. 'I didn't see you at Simba's presentation,' he growled.

'That was *today*?' Scar asked innocently. 'It must have slipped my mind.'

'As the King's brother, you should have been first in line at the ceremony!' Zazu squawked.

'I was first in line until that little hairball was born,' muttered Scar.

Mufasa leaned towards his brother. 'That little hairball is my son . . . and your future King.' He turned to Zazu. 'What am I going to do with him?' he said, sighing, as Scar padded off.

Chapter Two

'Dad!' Simba climbed on to his
sleeping father and roared in his ear.
'We've got to go! Wake up!'

'OK.' Mufasa yawned widely. 'I'm up.'

Sarabi smiled as she watched Mufasa
and their son set off towards Pride Rock.
Then she settled down again to sleep.

'Everything the sunlight touches is our
kingdom,' Mufasa explained, as he and
Simba stood on top of the rock and
watched the sun rise over the plains.

'One day, Simba, the sun will set on my time here and will rise with you as the new King.'

'And all this will be mine?' Simba asked, wide-eyed.

Mufasa nodded. 'Everything the light touches.'

Simba screwed up his eyes in the morning sunshine as he noticed a dark, shadowy place some distance off. 'What about that?' he said.

'That's beyond our borders,' Mufasa replied sternly. 'Never go there.'

At that moment, Zazu swooped down to join them. 'Good morning, sire,' he squawked. 'Just checking in with the morning report. There are hyenas prowling the Pride Lands.'

Mufasa looked angry. 'Take Simba home,' he told Zazu.

'Dad!' Simba looked disappointed as Mufasa loped off across the plains. 'Can't I come too?'

'No, son.' Mufasa did not stop.

'I never get to go anywhere,' Simba complained to Zazu.

'Young master,' Zazu replied sternly, 'one day you will be King. Then you can chase those stupid, mangy poachers from dawn to dusk.'

Simba still looked cross. He didn't want to wait until he was grown up to chase hyenas! Then he spotted his uncle, Scar, slinking along a cliff ledge. Simba bounded over to join him.

'Hey, Uncle Scar, guess what?' Simba beamed.

'I despise guessing games,' Scar snapped.

'I'm going to be King of Pride Rock!' Simba laughed. 'My dad just showed me the whole kingdom.'

'Oh, goody,' replied Scar sulkily.

'Uncle Scar, when I'm King, what does that make you?' Simba enquired with interest.

'A monkey's uncle,' muttered Scar. 'So your father showed you the whole kingdom?'

'Everything,' Simba boasted.

Scar's eyes narrowed cunningly. 'Including what's over the hill at the northern border?' he asked silkily.

'Well, no,' Simba admitted. 'He said I couldn't go there.'

'And he's absolutely right.' Scar shot

his nephew a sideways glance. 'It's too dangerous. Only the bravest lions can go there.'

'I'm brave!' Simba said indignantly. 'What's there?'

Scar shook his head. 'I can't tell you.'

'Why not?' Simba wanted to know.

'Simba, an elephants' graveyard is no place for a young prince,' Scar said solemnly. 'Oops, I've already said too much.' He stared hard at Simba. 'Now, promise me you'll *never* visit that dreadful place.'

'No problem,' Simba agreed jauntily. But he had already decided that he was going to visit the elephants' graveyard that very day.

'Good.' Scar smiled, showing all his sharp, white teeth. 'It'll be our little secret.'

Chapter Three

Simba ran off immediately to find his friend Nala. He wanted her to join him on his great adventure to the elephants' graveyard.

The lionesses were lying around, watching their children play, and Nala was being groomed by her mother, Sarafina.

'Hey, Nala.' Simba bounced over to her. 'Come with me. I know a *great* place we can go.'

'It's time for you to be groomed,'

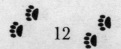

Sarabi, Simba's mother told him, and began licking his mane.

Simba pulled away impatiently. 'OK, I'm clean,' he said. 'Can we go now?'

'Where?' Nala asked.

'Er – near the water hole,' Simba replied, saying the first thing that came into his head.

Nala frowned. 'What's so great about the water hole?' she wanted to know.

'I'll tell you when we get there,' Simba whispered.

'Mum, can I go with Simba?' Nala asked Sarafina.

The lioness looked at Sarabi, who nodded.

'As long as Zazu goes with you,' she said.

Simba was dismayed when Zazu flew down to join them. They'd have to get away from him somehow.

'Where are we really going?' Nala whispered as the three of them set off.

'To the elephants' graveyard,' Simba replied.

Zazu, who couldn't hear what they were talking about, watched them with their heads together and chuckled happily. 'Just look at you two,' he said. 'Your parents will be thrilled, seeing as you are going to be married.'

Simba stopped and stared at Zazu. 'I can't marry her,' he gasped. 'She's my friend.'

'You've got no choice,' Zazu replied briskly. 'Marriage between your two

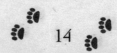

14

families is a tradition.'

'When I'm King, that'll be the first tradition to go,' Simba muttered. Then he began to hum to himself, and finally to sing aloud: 'Oh, I just can't wait to be King!'

As they went on their way, animals of all kinds heard Simba singing and they came out to meet their future King. They joined in the dancing and singing, and when a large hippopotamus accidentally sat on Zazu, Simba and Nala seized their chance and ran off without him.

'I beg your pardon, madam,' Zazu gasped, trying to pull his feathers free, 'but do get off!'

The hornbill finally pushed the hippo away and then looked around anxiously. The two lion cubs were nowhere to be seen.

'Simba!' Zazu squawked. 'Nala! Where are you?'

Chapter Four

'All right!' Simba said eagerly. 'We've lost him. I'm a genius!'

Nala pounced on him. 'Hey, it was my idea!'

The two lion cubs wrestled playfully together. They rolled over and over, tumbling down a hill, and then came to an abrupt halt at the bottom. They suddenly found themselves in a dark, shadowy, lonely place. The earth was black, steam rose from a jagged ravine and ivory tusks lay littered about. They realized that this must be the elephants' graveyard.

Nala shivered. 'It's really creepy.'

'Isn't it great?' Simba said. He walked over to a large elephant skull. 'I wonder if its brain's still in there?'

Suddenly Zazu swooped down in front of them. 'We're way beyond the Pride Lands boundary!' he squawked furiously. 'And right now we're in very real danger!'

'I laugh in the face of danger,' Simba said scornfully. But then he nearly jumped out of his skin as a loud cackle of evil laughter sounded behind him. Three hyenas slunk out of a cave and fixed him with an ugly stare.

'Well, Banzai,' sneered Shenzi, 'what have we here?'

'I don't know,' Banzai giggled. 'What do you think, Ed?'

Ed roared with laughter.

'Just what I was thinking.' Banzai grinned. 'A trio of trespassers!'

'Quite by accident, I assure you,' Zazu broke in hastily.

Shenzi's eyes narrowed. 'Wait, I know you. You're Mufasa's little stooge.'

Banzai turned to Simba. 'So that makes you the future King,' he cackled.

'You can't do anything to me,' Simba said bravely.

'Actually, they can,' Zazu admitted. 'We're on their land.' He glanced up at the sky. 'Well, look at the sun,' he blustered. 'Time to go.'

'Oh, do stick around for dinner,' Shenzi

laughed. 'Make mine a cub sandwich!'

Simba, Nala and Zazu made a run for it, but the hyenas were constantly snapping at their heels. They caught Zazu, just as Simba and Nala managed to scramble up on top of a ridge.

'Where's Zazu?' Simba asked.
He and Nala peered over the ridge in time to see the hornbill being dunked in a pot of boiling water. Luckily, an explosion from under the pot sent him flying up into the sky and he was free.

'Pick on somebody your own size!' Simba yelled at the hyenas.

'Like you?' Shenzi replied, and with that the three hyenas leapt towards Simba and Nala.

Panting, Simba and Nala ran for their

lives. They managed to scramble up a
pile of bleached white bones and down
the other side again. But the hyenas were
always close behind and they weren't
giving up. They finally cornered the two
terrified lion cubs in the ravine and stood
grinning at them.

'Here, kitty,' Banzai called.

Simba drew himself up and tried to
roar at the hyenas. But he could manage
only a tiny sound. The hyenas rolled
around, laughing.

'Do it again!' Shenzi giggled.

'RRRRRROOOOOOOAAAAARRRRR!'
This time the ferocious growl echoed
loudly around the cave. Mufasa leapt
towards the terrified hyenas, knocking

them all to the ground.

'We're sorry,' Shenzi babbled as Mufasa stood over them.

'If you ever come near my son again . . .' The King stared furiously at the cowering hyenas, and then led Simba, Nala and Zazu away.

'Dad,' Simba began awkwardly, feeling very ashamed of himself, 'I'm sorry.'

'Zazu, take Nala home,' Mufasa ordered gravely. 'I have to teach my son a lesson.'

Mufasa waited until Zazu and Nala had gone, then he turned to Simba. 'I'm very disappointed in you,' he said. 'You disobeyed me and put Nala in danger.'

Simba hung his head. 'I just wanted to be brave like you.'

'I'm only brave when I have to be,'

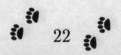

Mufasa explained. Then he smiled at his son. 'Come here.'

Simba rushed over to his father and they rolled around together happily for a few moments.

'We'll always be together, Dad, right?' Simba asked.

Mufasa pointed up at the night sky. 'Look at the stars, Simba,' he said. 'The great kings of the past look down on us from those stars. So whenever you feel alone, just remember that those kings are there to guide you. And so am I.'

Back in the elephants' graveyard, the hyenas were lying around complaining.

'That Mufasa!' Shenzi snapped. 'I won't be able to sit down for a week! If it weren't for those lions, we'd be running the place.'

'I hate lions,' Banzai muttered. 'They're ugly and they smell.'

'Surely we lions are not all bad?' purred a voice behind them.

The hyenas jumped up. Scar was sitting on top of the cliff, looking down at them.

'Oh, Scar, it's you,' said Banzai. 'You're our friend.'

'Charmed,' replied Scar. He threw a large piece of meat down to the hyenas, who pounced on it hungrily. 'Now, be prepared.'

'For what?' Banzai asked. 'The death of the king?'

Scar smiled widely. 'What a good idea! Killing Mufasa and Simba, would make me King!'

Chapter Five

'Now, you wait here.' Scar sat Simba down on a large rock in the middle of the gorge. 'Your father has a marvellous surprise for you!'

Simba looked excited. 'What is it?'

'If I told you, it wouldn't be a surprise,' Scar replied. 'I'll go and get him now.'

Scar slunk away to the edge of the overhanging cliff. The three hyenas, Banzai, Shenzi and Ed, were crouched below, hungrily watching a herd of wildebeest grazing quietly on the plains.

'There he is!' Shenzi spotted Scar above them. That was the hyenas' signal. They jumped to their feet and began to move stealthily towards the herd.

Meanwhile, Simba was growing bored waiting for his father to arrive. He decided to practise roaring as loudly as he could.

'GRRRRRRRRRRRR!' he growled, opening his mouth wide.

The noise echoed round the gorge. It really *did* sound louder, Simba thought proudly. Then he frowned. Why was the noise getting louder – and louder?

The sound of thundering hooves filled the air all around the lion cub. Suddenly hundreds of wildebeest appeared at the rim of the gorge. They all plunged over the edge and down the slope into the narrow ravine. The hyenas, who had frightened the wildebeest into stampeding, were chasing along behind them, biting at their tails. The big animals, with their sharp, curved horns, were heading straight towards Simba.

'Quick!' Scar rushed up to Mufasa, who was chatting with Zazu. 'Stampede in the gorge! Simba's down there!'

'Simba?' Mufasa asked anxiously. The next moment he was on his feet, racing for the gorge.

Zazu flew on ahead and spotted Simba clinging desperately to a tree as the wildebeest stampeded past him, kicking up clouds of dust.

'Zazu, help me!' Simba cried.

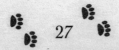

'Your father's on his way!' Zazu squawked.

Mufasa ran down the side of the gorge with Scar behind him. He leapt into the middle of the herd, fighting his way through the wildebeest. Several times he was knocked off his feet and almost trampled, but still the big lion battled on towards his son.

'Oh, this is awful!' Zazu moaned to Scar. 'I'm going to get help.' But one big swipe of Scar's powerful paw sent the hornbill spinning through the air. He crashed against a rock and lay there, dazed.

Suddenly a wildebeest smashed into the tree Simba was clinging to. The lion cub was tossed high into the air and somersaulted over the top of the frightened animals. As he fell to the

Rafiki lifted Simba high into the air.

The animals bowed low to the lion cub.

*'That little hairball is my son ... and your future king!' Mufa...
growled.*

'What have we here?' Banzai grinned. 'A trio of trespassers!'

Mufasa knocked the terrified hyenas to the ground.

never you feel alone, look at the stars, Simba.'

'Zazu, help me!' Simba cried.

'What have you done, Simba?' Scar asked.

'Timon!' squealed Pumbaa. 'She's going to eat me!'

'Simba, you have forgotten me!'

'The choice is yours, Scar,' Simba roared. 'Either step down or fig

They knew one day they would stand here with their son.

ground, Mufasa leapt forward and caught his son safely in his mouth. Fighting his way through the herd, he hauled Simba up on to a rocky ledge and out of danger.

'Dad!' Simba called frantically, as Mufasa hurled himself at the cliff. The lion tried to dig his claws into the rock and climb higher, but every second he was slowly sliding back towards the wildebeest.

Mufasa looked up at Scar, who was standing over him. 'Brother!' he cried. 'Help me!'

Scar leaned over, but instead of helping Mufasa, he dug his claws fiercely into the lion's paws. 'Long live the King!' he hissed.

Scar flung Mufasa off the cliff and the lion was carried away by the stampeding herd.

'Dad!' Simba whimpered. He hadn't seen what his uncle had done, but he knew that his father was in danger. 'Dad!'

The wildebeest had gone, leaving nothing behind them but clouds of dust. Choking back sobs, Simba climbed down from the ledge and hurried to find his father. Mufasa lay under a tree, his body battered and broken, his eyes closed.

'Dad?' Simba sobbed. 'Wake up!'

'What have you done, Simba?' Scar asked innocently, padding towards him.

'It was an accident,' Simba replied tearfully, gazing down at his dead father.

'Of course it was,' Scar said silkily.

'But what will your mother think?'

Simba looked frightened. 'What shall I do?'

'Run away,' Scar told him firmly, 'and never return!'

Simba was too upset and frightened to think clearly. He took to his heels immediately and set off across the plains. Scar turned to the hyenas, who had sidled over. 'Kill him,' he ordered.

Laughing, the hyenas ran after the lion cub. Simba saw them coming and tried to escape, but he slipped from the rocky ledge and plunged into a thicket full of thorns. The hyenas came to a dead stop and looked at each other.

'Get him!' Banzai said.

'I'm not going in there!' Shenzi

snapped. 'I'll come out looking like a cactus! And anyway –' the hyena smiled sleekly – 'he's as good as dead out there in the desert.'

Chapter Six

'**G**et out of here!'

The meerkat rushed across the desert, waving his arms in the air. A group of buzzards was circling around the body of a young lion cub lying on the sand. The birds flew off, grumbling, as the meerkat dashed towards them. A large, fat warthog waddled along behind him.

'Hey, Timon,' the warthog announced suddenly. 'I think this one's still alive!'

Timon bent over the cub, looking alarmed. 'Hey, Pumbaa, it's a lion!' he gasped. Run!'

'It's just a little lion,' replied Pumbaa, staring down at Simba. 'And he's all alone.'

Timon sighed. 'OK, let's go and find some shade.'

They picked Simba up and carried him gently to the nearest oasis, where they laid him underneath a tree. Timon splashed some water on to the lion cub's face and heard him moan faintly.

'You OK, kid?' Timon asked as Simba opened his eyes.

'I guess so,' Simba replied groggily. He climbed unsteadily to his feet and turned away. 'Thanks for helping me.'

'Hey, where are you going?' Timon wanted to know.

'What's the matter?' Pumbaa asked. 'Where are you from?'

'Who cares?' Simba said sadly. 'I can never go back.'

Timon nodded wisely. 'You know, kid,' he said, 'when the world turns its back on you, just turn your back on the world.'

Simba shook his head. 'That's not what I was taught.'

'Then maybe you need a new lesson,' Timon broke in. '*Hakuna matata*.'

'It means no worries,' Pumbaa added. 'For the rest of your days.'

Simba listened thoughtfully as Pumbaa and Timon danced around him, singing *hakuna matata*. It all sounded wonderful. A simple, easy life with no worries . . .

*

'Man, I'm stuffed!' Simba yawned. He rolled over and grinned at Timon and Pumbaa.

Many months had passed and Simba was now a fully grown lion, almost as big and strong as Mufasa had been. But he'd never returned to the Pride Lands. Simba had put all thoughts of his father and mother, Zazu, Nala and everyone else back home firmly out of his mind. Now his family were Timon and Pumbaa.

'Me too,' Pumbaa chimed in. 'I ate like a pig.'

'You *are* a pig!' Simba pointed out, and they all laughed.

Pumbaa looked up at the night sky, which was dotted with silver stars. 'You ever wonder what those sparkly dots up there are?' he asked dreamily.

Simba frowned as a memory flashed into his mind. 'Someone once told me,' he began, 'that the great kings of the past are up there, watching over us.'

'Who told you that?' Timon asked.

Simba shrugged, looking embarrassed. 'Pretty dumb, huh?' He got slowly to his feet and padded over to the cliff edge. There he slumped down, sending leaves and seed pods drifting up into the air, and he stared out over the valley.

Deep in the heart of the Pride Lands morning was breaking. Rafiki the old baboon sat silently in his tree. Since Scar had returned to tell them of the terrible deaths of Mufasa and Simba, everything had gone wrong. Scar had become King, but he had no interest in the duties and responsibilities that were part of the job. He ruled with the help of the hyenas, who had taken over the Pride Lands. There was no food or water and the animals were starving. Mufusa's kingdom was no longer green and lush, but was becoming darker and more deserted by the day.

Suddenly Rafiki sat up and sniffed the air. A cloud of leaves and seed pods was drifting towards him. The old baboon caught a handful and sniffed. Then his face brightened at the familiar scent.

'Simba's alive!' he said joyfully.

Chapter Seven

Pumbaa was stalking a very tasty-looking bug along the ground. He was just getting close enough to snap it up when he heard a branch crack behind him. Suddenly on his guard, the warthog glanced round and saw a young lioness flying through the trees towards him.

'Timon!' Pumbaa squealed in fright as he fled, with the lioness snapping at his heels.

The warthog was so scared that he didn't look where he was going. He ran

straight under a big tree root and got stuck halfway.

'Timon,' he roared as his friend appeared, 'she's going to eat me!'

The lioness was preparing to spring, her teeth drawn back in a snarl. But as Timon heaved desperately at Pumbaa's backside, trying to push him out, Simba suddenly leapt from the trees and threw himself at the lioness. Growling and snarling, they rolled over and over, until suddenly Simba stared up into the lioness's face.

'Nala?' he asked, his eyes wide.

Puzzled, Nala stared down at him. 'Who are *you*?'

'It's me – Simba!' Simba cried.

'Simba?' Nala could hardly believe her

ears. 'But how –'

The two lions leapt to their feet and nuzzled each other lovingly.

'Timon! Pumbaa!' Simba turned to his friends as Pumbaa finally managed to pull himself free. 'This is Nala.'

'Pleased to meet you,' said Nala, smiling. She turned happily to Simba. 'Wait till everyone finds out you're alive – especially your mother!'

Simba looked uneasy. 'She doesn't have to know,' he muttered. 'No one does.'

Nala was shocked. 'But they think you're dead! Scar told us about the stampede.'

'What else did he tell you?' Simba asked warily.

'What else matters?' Nala retorted.

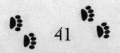

'You're alive and you're the King!'

Timon and Pumbaa stared open-mouthed at Simba.

'No,' Simba said quickly. 'I'm not the King. I was going to be, but that was a long time ago.'

'Could you excuse us for a minute?' Nala said to Timon and Pumbaa. She waited until they'd moved away before turning back to Simba and nuzzling him affectionately. 'I've really missed you,' she said.

'They're going to fall in love,' Timon whispered to Pumbaa.

'You've been alive all this time,' Nala went on. 'Why didn't you come back to Pride Rock?'

'I needed to live my own life,' Simba

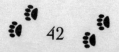

replied awkwardly. 'And I'm not the King anyway. Scar is.'

Nala looked sad. 'He has let the hyenas take over the Pride Lands,' she told Simba. 'Everything's destroyed. There's no food or water. He keeps Zazu in a cage and won't take advice from anyone. You must do something, or everyone will starve.'

'I can't,' Simba said helplessly, hanging his head. 'You don't understand. *Hakuna matata*. It means there's nothing you can do about it, so why worry?'

'What's happened to you?' Nala asked, suddenly sounding cross. 'You're not the Simba I remember.'

'Don't tell me how to live my life,' Simba snapped. 'You don't know what

I've been through.'

'I would if you told me.'

'Forget it!' Simba roared furiously.

'Fine!' Nala retorted, and with that she ran off through the trees.

Chapter Eight

'She's wrong,' Simba told himself as he padded along. 'I can't go back. You can't change the past.'

An old baboon was sitting in a tree overhead. As Simba passed by, he shook the branches and began to sing. Simba glanced up, irritated.

'Will you cut it out?' he growled.

'The question is,' Rafiki said thoughtfully, 'who are you?'

'I'm not sure now.' Simba sighed.

Rafiki grinned at him. 'I know who you

are,' he said. 'You're Mufasa's boy.'

Simba was shocked. He stared at the old baboon, not knowing what to say. Rafiki shrugged.

'Bye,' he called, and scurried off.

Simba found his voice at last. 'Wait!' he called, loping after the baboon. 'You knew my father?'

'I *know* your father,' Rafiki corrected him. 'He's not dead.'

Simba's face lit up with joy.

'Follow me and I'll show him to you,' Rafiki ordered.

Simba could hardly keep up with the baboon as he swung his way through the trees. Rafiki stopped on a rocky outcrop that hung over a crystal-clear pool. 'Look down there,' he said.

Simba peered cautiously into the water. But to his disappointment, he could see nothing but his own reflection. 'That's not my father,' he muttered.

'Look harder.'

Simba stared down at himself. Suddenly his reflection began to blur and change until it became Mufasa's face.

'You see?' Rafiki said gently. 'He lives in you.'

'Simba.'

Simba's eyes widened as he recognized Mufasa's voice. 'Father?' he stammered, lifting his head and looking up into the sky.

The clouds above the lion's head were moving. As Simba watched, they swirled and shifted and became the shape of a lion.

'Simba,' Mufasa said gravely, looking down at his son, 'you have forgotten me.'

'No,' Simba gasped, staring upwards. 'How could I?'

'You have forgotten who you are, and so forgotten me,' replied Mufasa. 'You must take your place in the circle of life.' Golden sunlight swirled through the clouds. 'Remember, you are my son and the one true King.' Mufasa's image began to fade. 'Remember . . .'

'Dad!' Simba shouted. 'Please don't leave me!'

But Mufasa had vanished.

Shaking his mane, Simba turned to Rafiki. 'I know what I must do,' he said sadly, 'but going back means facing my past – OUCH!'

Rafiki had just tapped Simba firmly on the head with his staff.

'What was that for?' Simba grumbled, rubbing his head.

'It doesn't matter,' Rafiki said with a grin. 'It's in the past!'

'Yeah, but it still hurts!' Simba snapped.

'Well, you can either run from the past,' Rafiki replied, 'or you can learn from it.' He hit out at Simba again, but this time the lion ducked and sped off.

'Where are you going?' Rafiki called.

'I'm going back!' Simba roared.

Chapter Nine

'Wake up!'

Timon, who was snoozing happily next to Pumbaa, yawned and opened his eyes. He almost jumped out of his skin when he saw a lioness standing next to him.

'It's me,' Nala said quickly, as Pumbaa leapt up too. 'Have you seen Simba?'

'You won't find him here,' a voice overhead answered with a chuckle.

They looked up to see Rafiki crouched in the tree above them. 'The King has returned,' the baboon told them.

Nala's eyes widened. 'He's gone back,' she gasped.

'Hey, what's going on?' Timon demanded.

'Simba must fight his uncle, Scar, to claim his place as King,' Nala explained.

Simba stood on top of a rocky cliff and looked across the Pride Lands. He could hardly believe that this was the same beautiful green place he had run away from all those months ago. Now the land was bare and barren. The trees were blackened and twisted, and heaps of bleached white bones lay everywhere. Small fires burned here and there, and in the distance Simba could see Pride Rock. A large group of hyenas was lounging around the base of it.

'Simba!' Nala padded along the cliff to join him. 'It's awful, isn't it?'

'It's my kingdom,' Simba replied. 'If I don't fight for it, who will?'

'I will,' Nala said firmly, as Timon and Pumbaa appeared behind her.

'At your service, my liege.' Pumbaa bowed low.

'If it's important to you, Simba, we're with you to the end,' Timon added.

They set off across the dark and deserted plain towards Pride Rock. They stopped before they got too close and peered over a fallen tree trunk at the lazy hyenas.

'You guys have got to create a diversion,' Simba whispered to Timon and Pumbaa.

'How?' Timon asked. 'Dressing up in women's clothes and doing the hula?'

That was exactly what Simba had in mind. A few minutes later, Timon and Pumbaa rushed out in front of the hyenas, with Timon dressed in a grass skirt. 'If you're hungry for juicy fat meat, eat Pumbaa, for he is a treat!' Timon sang, pointing at the fat warthog.

The hyenas leapt to their feet. Chuckling, they raced after Timon and Pumbaa, who ran for their lives. Immediately Simba and Nala hurried towards Pride Rock.

'Fetch my mother and rally the lionesses,' Simba whispered. But then he heard his uncle's voice.

'Sarabi!'

Simba swung round to see his mother making her way through the army of hyenas that surrounded Scar. She walked with dignity, her head held high, ignoring them. Simba watched as she stopped before Scar.

'Your hunting party isn't doing its job,' Scar snarled.

'There's no food,' Sarabi said quietly. 'We must leave Pride Rock.'

'Never!' Scar roared furiously.

Sarabi looked at him with contempt. 'If you were half the King that Mufasa was,' she began.

But she got no further. Scar's huge paw shot out and hit her. Sarabi flew through the air and landed on the rocky ground.

With a growl of outrage, Simba

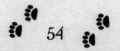

bounded from his hiding place. Scar and the hyenas gasped when they saw him, but Simba had eyes for no one but his mother.

'Mufasa?' Sarabi peered groggily up at her son.

'No, it's me,' Simba said, nuzzling his mother lovingly. 'Simba.'

'Simba!' Scar muttered, looking horrified. He quickly gathered his wits about him. 'I'm a little surprised to see you *alive*.'

Shenzi, Banzai and Ed slunk guiltily into the shadows.

'The choice is yours, Scar,' Simba said grimly, as Nala appeared with the other lionesses. 'Either step down or fight.'

Scar smiled an evil smile. 'Tell them

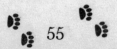

who was responsible for Mufasa's death,' he suggested.

Simba turned to the lionesses. 'I am,' he admitted.

'Murderer!' Scar roared.

'But it was an accident,' Simba broke in.

'You're in trouble again,' Scar smirked, backing Simba to the edge of the rock.

Simba tumbled over, but he managed to hang on by his claws. Below him a volcano boiled and smoked.

'But this time Daddy isn't here to save you,' Scar sneered, leaning over Simba, who was desperately trying to haul himself up the rocky cliff face. 'Now this looks familiar,' he mused. 'This is just the way your father looked – before I killed him!'

Chapter Ten

With a roar of fury, Simba somehow found the strength to hurl himself upwards and land on top of Scar.

'Murderer!' he growled. 'Tell them!'

The lionesses pressed forward.

'All right,' Scar choked, Simba's paw pressing at his throat. 'I killed Mufasa!'

The lionesses gasped. Suddenly the hyenas that had been lurking in the shadows surged forward and attacked Simba, allowing Scar to break free. Immediately the lionesses leapt into action, helped by Timon and Pumbaa. Rafiki also joined in, hitting the hyenas with his staff.

Simba chased Scar along Pride Rock.

'Murderer!' he roared again, as he cornered his uncle.

Scar cowered against the rock 'But it was the hyenas' idea!' he protested. 'They are our enemies!' As he spoke, he didn't realize that Shenzi, Banzai and Ed were nearby, listening to every word.

'Run away, Scar,' Simba growled sternly. 'And never return.'

'Oh, of course,' Scar agreed. He slunk past Simba, then turned quickly to flick some fiery embers into his nephew's face with his paw. Simba roared with pain, but as Scar leapt at him, he managed to flip the lion over the edge of the rock. Scar landed heavily at the bottom, in the middle of a large pack of hyenas.

'Ah, my friends,' Scar said nervously, as the hyenas closed in.

'Friends?' Shenzi turned to Banzai. 'I thought he said we were the enemy?'

Ed laughed and licked his lips. Scar screamed with fear as the hyenas closed in on him and attacked.

The rains had started to fall on the parched land. High up on Pride Rock, Rafiki turned to Simba. 'It is time,' he said, beaming.

Simba embraced the old baboon. Then he padded to the edge of the rock to look out over his kingdom. And he knew that one day very soon, when the Pride Lands were green and beautiful again, he and Nala would stand there with their son, and Mufasa, with all the other kings in the skies, would be smiling down on them.